MIRANDA and the CAT

MIRANDA
and the CAT

by Linell Smith

Illustrated by PEGGY BACON

Little, Brown and Company
Boston   Toronto

J

c. 2

C L

Published simultaneously in Canada
by Little, Brown & Company (Canada) Limited

PRINTED IN THE UNITED STATES OF AMERICA

For Nell, Francie, and Biddy

ONCE THERE WAS a Cat. He was not a fat cat. He was not the lap-sitting kind of cat. He was a thin cat; so thin that you could count his bones. This Cat was marked with the scars of many battles. He lived in a turned-over box behind a garbage can in the alley of a big city. In fact, he was an alley cat. And proud of it.

The Cat was boss of all the streets and alleys for ten blocks around. The other cats kept out of his way and most dogs ran from him. Once in a while, though, a very bold dog might start a fight. Pity the poor dog! The Cat's claws were sharp. His eye was keen. He really was a marvelous fighter. The dog would be lucky to get off without serious harm and it would never try to fight the Cat again.

Actually, the Cat seldom fought any more. None of the animals he knew cared to argue with him. As for people, the Cat left them strictly alone. He had no use for them.

The Cat might never have known people at all if it hadn't been for a tennis ball. One warm summer morning the ball came bouncing in behind the garbage can and rolled to rest beside the Cat's box home. The Cat arched his back and spat at it. But the object did not seem dangerous after all, so he lay down again for his morning nap.

The ball had been thrown by Miranda. Miranda

had straight brown hair and a solemn face. She was almost as skinny as the Cat. She lived in the ground-floor apartment of one of the buildings on the alley. Her two older brothers were playing baseball on a vacant lot a few blocks away. Miranda loved base-ball and had asked if she could play too. But Tim had answered, "Nope. No girls allowed."

So she had stayed behind. She waited until the boys were out of sight and then took her precious tennis ball from her top bureau drawer. It was an old, waterlogged ball, but Miranda loved it. She went out in the alley and started practicing pitches against the fence. She aimed for an old poster on the fence.

Usually, Miranda hit the poster almost every time. But this morning her pitching was rather wild. She was trying to master the knuckle ball and couldn't seem to get the hang of it. She began to lose her temper. At last, after she had missed the target ten times in a row, she grabbed the ball and hurled it furiously at nothing in particular. It hit the nearest telephone pole and bounced down the alley. Then it disappeared from sight behind a pile of garbage cans and trash.

Miranda scampered after it. She didn't want to lose it. She poked at the trash cautiously. She had sometimes seen rats in the alley and she was afraid of rats. But when no rats appeared, she became bolder. She moved a garbage can and looked behind it. She saw a partly turned-over box. Next to the box was the ball. She reached down to pick it up and as she did so, she looked in the box. The Cat looked back at her steadily. Miranda forgot about the ball. She loved cats. She knelt down beside the box and said softly, "Hello, Cat."

The Cat's expression did not change, but his back arched slightly. His ears flattened against his head. Miranda put her hand out very slowly to pat him. The Cat gathered himself together and sprang forward, his claws extended. He raked her arm in passing and then in another bound he cleared the alley fence and was gone.

Miranda sat back on her heels, holding her bleeding arm. She had wanted to make friends. What had she done wrong? She picked up the ball and walked sadly back down the alley. When she got home she looked in the bathroom medicine cabinet for something to put on her scratches. Her mother came in. She stared at Miranda's arm and said, "What in the world happened to you, Miranda? Here, let me see." She took out a bottle of Mercurochrome.

Miranda told her about the Cat.

"He was frightened of you," her mother said. "Alley cats are very wild and they are frightened of being hurt."

"I guess maybe that was partly it," said Miranda, "but I felt that he was mad at me too. He acted insulted — like a king or something."

Her mother laughed. "Well, if you really want to make friends with the Cat, darling, I'll let you have the scraps from the table tonight. I'm sure that the quickest way to his heart is through his stomach."

And so when the Cat came home that night, he found some food and milk there. The Cat was puzzled and quite suspicious. This seemed dangerous. He circled the strange gifts cautiously. At last, however, he settled down to eat. It was the best meal he had had in a very long time.

Every day after that, Miranda brought the scraps to the box in the alley. She never saw the Cat, but the food was always eaten.

Once Miranda was later than usual. There had been company for dinner and more dishes to wash. She hurried to the box home and put the food down quickly. As she turned to go, she felt that she was being watched. She glanced around and saw a pair of pale green eyes. They stared at her from the darkness. She started towards them, but they disappeared at once.

From then on she knew that when she brought food, the Cat was watching her.

But one evening, late in July, something happened. Miranda stayed awhile after she brought the food. She wanted to see the Cat eat if she could. So she was there when the Cat dragged his torn and bleeding body over the fence. He fell with a soft thud at her feet. Miranda looked at the motionless bundle of fur in horror. She could hardly recognize the Cat because there was so much blood. But just then he

opened one eye. He looked at her very much the way he had when they first met.

"Impudence!" said the look. "How dare you stare at me! Look to your manners or I'll claw you!"

So Miranda knew it was the Cat. She gave a little sob and knelt down beside him. She quickly wrapped him in her old torn sweater. Then, carrying him as gently as she could, she hurried home.

When she arrived, her mother and brothers were watching television in the living room. They all looked up when she appeared in the doorway. Her mother asked swiftly, "What is it, darling? What's wrong?"

Miranda walked slowly over to the table and put her burden down. "It's the Cat," she said in a small, strained voice. "I think he's almost dead."

They all crowded around then. Her mother pulled back a corner of the bloody sweater. The Cat lay there before their curious eyes. He could do nothing about it. He was too weak.

"Whew!" whistled Tim. "He's *had* it!"

"You're not kidding," said Joey, the oldest brother.

"Don't look at him," begged Miranda. "He doesn't like it."

"Well for Pete's sake, who do you think he is, the King of England?" drawled Tim.

"No, honestly, I mean it," pleaded Miranda. "He doesn't like people at all and I think it's horrid to stand so close to him and stare when he's helpless. I just brought him here because — oh, I don't really know. I guess it was because it was so dark out and it seemed sad to me to die in the dark."

She began to cry miserably.

"Gee, Sis," said Tim awkwardly, "I didn't know you cared specially about that old cat. Don't cry. I'll stay away from him. Just stop crying, will you?"

"Oh, come on, Rannie," said Joey. "Tim and I won't bother the Cat any more. Cheer up."

Miranda's mother looked quietly at the Cat. He looked back at her with the proud gaze that Miranda knew so well.

"Miranda," she said slowly, "I don't think that this cat is doing to die. He looks to me as if he had a lot of will to live. If we help him a little, he may be all right."

"Oh, Mother!" said Miranda breathlessly. "I'll help him — just tell me what to do."

Her mother went to the cookie jar that stood on the mantel. Out of it she took four dollar bills. She put them in Miranda's pocket.

"Here, Rannie," she said, "I've been saving this for a rainy day. Take the money and the Cat down to Dr. Barton, the vet. I don't know if it's enough, but it's all we can spare. Maybe he'll help."

"Can we go too?" asked the boys.

"Yes," said their mother. "I don't want Rannie to be out by herself this late at night."

So Miranda gathered the Cat up in her arms and she and her brothers hurried down the dark streets in silence. At last they came to the veterinarian's office. The lights were still on. Through the window, they could see Dr. Barton in his white coat. They scurried up the steps and rang the bell.

Dr. Barton answered the door himself. "I'm sorry," he began, "I'm afraid office hours are — " But he never finished what he was going to say.

He looked down at three pairs of pleading eyes and said instead, "Won't you come in?"

They did. Joe and Tim looked at magazines while Miranda followed Dr. Barton into the examining room. Dr. Barton looked very solemn as he examined the Cat. The Cat was no help at all because he spat and scratched whenever he could. At last Dr. Barton looked at Miranda and said, "Is this your pet, little girl?"

"Not exactly," faltered Miranda. She suddenly found herself telling the veterinarian all about herself and the Cat.

When she had finished, Dr. Barton said, "I see. That's a very interesting story, young lady. I'll try my best to help you out, but this cat is pretty badly cut up. I think he must have been hit by a car."

Miranda reached in her pocket and pulled out the money her mother had given her. "Mother took this from the savings jar," she said timidly. "Will it be enough?"

The vet looked at her over his glasses. "That won't

be necessary at all," he said in a gruff voice. "I will handle this case free of charge. Now if you'll take a seat in the waiting room, I'll get to work."

Miranda went back to the boys. They looked up expectantly when she came in. "What did he say?" Tim asked.

"He wouldn't take the money," she said. "He's working on the Cat now, trying to save him."

"Gee," said Joey, "that's a good deal."

They sat in silence for a while. Then Tim said, "How long do you think he'll take, Rannie?"

"I don't know," said Miranda. "He did say that the Cat was hurt pretty badly, so I guess he'll take a good while."

Finally, after what seemed forever, the door of the examining room opened. Dr. Barton appeared, carrying the Cat. The animal was wrapped in bandages and looked furious.

"I've given him something to help the pain and to keep him quiet, so I think you can take him home now," he said to Miranda. "I've done all I can for

him. I can't give you much hope, though. He's been badly hurt and from what I know of this kind of cat, being penned up with people is just as bad for him as his injuries. However, I wish you luck."

Miranda gently took the cat from the vet. "Is there anything special I should do for him?" she asked.

"Yes," said Dr. Barton. "I have some ointment here. It should be put on the wounds every day, and his bandages should be changed when they become soiled. Those are two things that you can do. But the third thing is really the most important. You should leave him alone as much as possible. Try to make him feel that he hasn't lost his freedom."

"Thank you very much," said Miranda gratefully. "I'll try to do everything you said." She slipped the tube of ointment into her pocket. Then she and the boys started towards the door.

"Thanks again," they all said as they went out.

"You're welcome " answered Dr. Barton with a smile. "Don't forget to come again if you need help."

"We won't," promised Miranda.

When they got home, Miranda told their mother what had happened.

"And he wouldn't take the money, Mom," Joey added when his sister had finished the story.

"What a kind man he must be," she said. "Well, now we must think of a place to put the Cat."

"How about a box like the one he usually lives in?" suggested Miranda.

"That's a good idea," said her mother.

"I know where one is," Tim volunteered. He disappeared into his room. He came back with a wooden box so like the Cat's box home in the alley that it might have been its twin.

"But that's the box you keep your model airplanes

in," said Miranda, her eyes wide with surprise.

"Heck, I can just as well keep them in something else," Tim said in an offhand manner.

"Golly, Tim, thanks a lot!" said Miranda with a grateful smile.

"But where are you going to put the box?" asked Joey. "Where can he be alone the way the vet said?"

"I'll put it in my closet," Miranda decided. "I'll take the clothes out. It'll be dark and quiet in there and I don't think he'll mind it too much."

"Let me move the stuff for you," said Joey. "You have to hold the Cat." And he marched off to Miranda's room.

When Joey had moved her clothes and put the box in the closet, Miranda gently placed the Cat in his new bed. He glared at her, his green eyes steady and unblinking.

"I wish you wouldn't hate me so, Cat," said Miranda softly. "I just want to help. And I won't bother you any more than I have to."

But the Cat's expression did not change.

"I'll get you some warm milk," said Miranda. "I'm sure that would be good for you."

She ran to the kitchen and returned with the dish of milk. She put it down beside the Cat, where he could drink it without moving. "Good night," she whispered. She carefully shut the closet door. Then she undressed and got into bed.

Later, when her mother peeped into the room, Miranda was still awake.

"Mother?" she whispered.

"Yes, dear?" answered her mother.

"Do you think Cat will get well?" asked Miranda. "Do you think we can save him?"

"We can give him good care and hope for the best," said her mother gently.

"Yes, but he hates me so," said Miranda sadly. "He'll hate having me touch him when I change the bandages and put on the ointment. He'll fight me. And that will be bad for him because he's so weak."

"Rannie, darling," said her mother, "the Cat doesn't hate you really. What he hates is not being

free. I think that if you leave him completely alone except when you're doctoring him, he won't struggle enough to hurt himself."

"O.K.," said Miranda, "I'll do my best. Good night, Mother."

The next day when Miranda had finished the breakfast dishes, she fixed a dish of scraps and a saucer of milk for the Cat. She carried them into her room and set them on the chest of drawers. She opened the closet door quietly and looked in. The milk from last night was gone, she noticed, but the Cat was looking up at her fiercely.

"I'm sorry, Cat," she said, "but I have to put this ointment on now. I'll try not to hurt you, and I'll be as quick as I can."

When she picked him up, the Cat spat at her, but he didn't try to claw her. Perhaps he couldn't because he was so weak. At any rate, Miranda was encouraged. She began to unwrap his bandages very carefully. She gave a little gasp when she saw his wounds, but she went ahead firmly with the ointment. The Cat did not protest at all. Miranda bandaged him up again and put him back in his box. Then she placed the dishes of food and milk before him and said, "There you are, Cat. Thank you for being so good."

The Cat looked at her coldly and then lowered his eyelids in disdain. Miranda sighed as she closed the door.

Outside her room, her brothers were waiting for her. "How is he?" asked Tim eagerly.

"He's all right, I guess," said Miranda. "I can't quite understand him, though. I expected him to make a fuss when I put the ointment on and he didn't at all. And yet he hates me as much as ever. I can see it in his eyes."

"Maybe he's just smart," offered Joey. "Maybe he knows that you're helping him and that he'll just have to put up with you till he's well. But putting up with someone doesn't mean liking them."

"I think you're right," said Miranda slowly. "You know, I think that's just what he's doing."

And in the days that followed she was sure of it. The Cat let himself be bandaged and rebandaged with no complaint. He ate the food that was given him. He did not object when Miranda rubbed his wounds with the healing ointment. But he showed no signs of wanting to become friends.

Finally a day came when Miranda knew that the Cat didn't need bandages any more. His wounds had almost healed and he was beginning to prowl back and forth in the closet. After much thought, she decided to let him out in her room for a while.

When she opened the closet door, the Cat glanced up at her briefly and then stalked out into the room. He walked stiff-legged from one piece of furniture to another, sniffing, his tail a bottle brush of sus-

picion. At last, satisfied that there was nothing dangerous about, he sauntered back to Miranda and sat down.

"Meow," he said, fixing her with his stern green eyes.

"What do you want, Cat?" asked Miranda. She tried to keep the excitement out of her voice, but it was hard. She had never dreamed that he would come near her of his own free will.

The Cat twitched his tail lazily. "Prraouw," he remarked.

"I'll get you something to eat," said Miranda happily. "We're having fish for dinner and you can have the head."

She ran off to the kitchen and found her mother cleaning the fish.

"Can I have the head for the Cat?" she asked.

"Of course," said her mother. "How is he?"

"Fine," said Miranda. "Oh, Mother," she added joyfully, "he came over to me all on his own and spoke to me! He really did!"

"Why, Rannie, how wonderful!" exclaimed her mother. "I know how happy that makes you."

When Miranda returned to her room, the Cat was still sitting where she had left him. He looked up when she came in and Miranda thought, "Why, he almost looks as if he had accepted me. Not as a real friend, maybe, but at least I'm not an enemy any more."

She walked over and put the plate with the fish head on it down beside him on some old newspapers. "There, Cat," she said, "I think you'll like that."

The Cat did like it. He growled and snarled to himself as he ate the fish head. He dared anyone to try to take the tasty morsel away from him. When

he had finished, he licked his paws and washed his face carefully. Then he returned to his box in the closet and lay down for a snooze.

For the next few days, Miranda was very happy. Although the Cat was by no means affectionate, he behaved politely towards the little girl. Once or twice he was almost friendly.

But then he became very restless. He prowled back and forth endlessly. Often he would look at Miranda and give a harsh cry. It was more of a demand than anything else, and Miranda knew it. She also knew what it was that he wanted. For a while she pretended to herself that she didn't. Finally one evening she gave up. She sat down on the bed and watched him as he paced back and forth.

"Cat," she said in a small voice, "I'll do what you want, I promise I will. Only — are you sure? Please, won't you change your mind? After all, we're friends now and I love you very much."

The Cat turned and gazed at her with such longing in his eyes that Miranda sighed. "All right," she said.

"You're my very best friend and I want you to be happy."

She got up from the bed and walked slowly to the window. Then, squaring her shoulders, she firmly opened it.

Instantly the Cat sprang to the sill. He stood there a moment, almost as if he were thinking. Then with a "Prraouw" he leaped to the ground. He was soon out of sight, lost among the dim dark shapes of trash cans and rubbish.

A few minutes later, Tim found his sister stretched out on her bed, crying as if her heart would break. Then he saw the open window. Immediately he ran for his mother. "Oh, come quick," he begged. "I think the Cat's gone out the window, and Rannie's crying like anything!"

Together they went back to Miranda's room. They found her sitting up, wiping her tear-stained face on the hem of her dress.

"Rannie," said her mother softly, "Tim says that the Cat's run away — that he got out the window."

Miranda looked up at them slowly. "He *is* gone," she said, "but he didn't run away. I let him go."

"You *let* him go?" gasped Tim. "What in the world did you do that for?"

"I did it because I love him," said Miranda with a tiny sob.

"Well, of all the dumb things!" exploded Tim.

But Miranda's mother sat down on the bed and put her arms around the little girl. "You've made me very proud, Rannie," she said. "That was a very brave and loving thing to do."

"I don't understand," said Tim. "If Rannie loved that old cat so much, why did she let him go? And why was it a brave thing to do?"

"Because," said their mother, "when you really love something, you want it to be happy. The Cat wanted to be free. So Miranda gave him freedom, even though she knew that she would be very sad when he was gone."

"Oh," said Tim.

The weeks that followed were both happy and sad for Miranda. She discovered that the Cat had returned to his old home. So each night she faithfully brought him a dinner. The Cat was always waiting for her. She would stay with him for a while, sitting quietly on the garbage can beside the box and talking to him. They were friends now. The Cat seemed to look forward to her visits as much as she did. This made Miranda very happy indeed. But the sadness came when it was time to go. She would walk home slowly, wishing that somehow she could take her friend with her — or that he would come of his own free will. The Cat would watch her go, but he never followed her. He was home again now and he intended to stay there.

An evening came, however, when there was no Miranda. The Cat was puzzled. He waited patiently

for a while, then he went off in search of a rat that had run past the garbage cans. The next evening, he waited for her again, and again she failed him. One of the boys came with some food, but the Cat didn't trust him. He hid until the boy was gone.

And so it was the next night and the next. The Cat grew restless as the days passed. The little girl had become an important part of his life. So the Cat went in search of her.

He stalked down the alley until he came to a building which seemed familiar. He stopped there under an open window and listened. Suddenly he heard Miranda's voice.

"Cat," she was saying, "oh, Cat, I hope you're all right. I wish I could see you somehow and make sure."

The Cat's whiskers twitched. He understood none of his friend's words, but he knew now that she was in there. He sensed her unhappiness. The muscles in his powerful hind legs tensed for the spring to the window ledge. Yet he did not jump. The Cat was being torn between two strong feelings. The first was his sense of what was dangerous to his freedom. The second was his need for something that he had become used to — Miranda.

He waited there in the dark, his tail twisting nervously from side to side. Then the Cat made up his mind. He did something that for him was very brave. He leaped not only to the window ledge but down into the room itself — the room in which he had been a prisoner.

Miranda lay in her bed. Her face was pale and she had been crying. Beside her on the table were several bottles of pills and a thermometer in a glass of water.

But the Cat didn't notice any of these things. He had come to see his friend. He walked over to the bed and jumped lightly up beside Miranda.

"Prraouw," said the Cat. It could have meant only "Hello" or "Where have you been?" But to Miranda it meant everything important in the world.

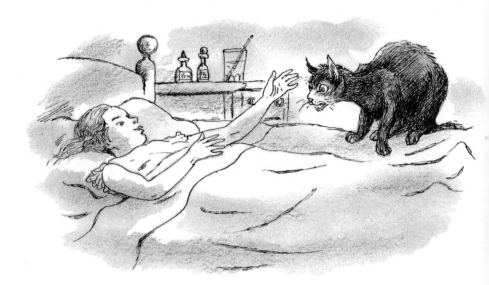

Her eyes grew wide and shining and she gathered him in her arms.

"Cat!" she said. "Oh, Cat! How glad I am to see you — and how lovely of you to come. I was so worried about you! Tim said that he never saw you when he brought your dinner. I was afraid that you might have been hurt again. I couldn't come to look for you myself because I've been quite sick, you see. Oh, Cat, I love you so!"

"Prrmm," said the Cat. And he settled down in his friend's arms and went to sleep.

Later, when Miranda's mother came into the room with the doctor, Miranda was sitting up in bed. Beside her was the Cat.

"Why, Rannie!" cried her mother in astonishment. "Isn't that the Cat?"

"Yes!" said Miranda excitedly. "Oh, Mother, isn't it wonderful? Think how hard it must have been for him to come into the house. But he did — because we're friends."

"Well," said the doctor with a smile, "so this is the

Cat I've heard so much about. I can't say he's much to look at, but it seems he's a pretty good doctor. Why, you're a different girl from the one I saw yesterday. How do you feel?"

"Just fine," said Miranda.

"Good," said the doctor. Then he looked down her throat, listened to her chest with his stethoscope, and took her temperature. When he read the thermometer, he laughed and said, "I guess I'll have to find myself a new patient. You're about cured. I think one more day in bed ought to do the trick.

"Take good care of your mistress," he said to the Cat as he turned to go.

"Oh, he's not *my* cat," said Miranda quickly.

"Not your cat?" asked the doctor, surprised.

"No," said Miranda, smiling and stroking the Cat gently. "He doesn't belong to anyone. He just belongs to himself. He's a very independent sort of cat. I kept him here and took care of him when he was sick. And now that *I'm* sick, he's come back to take care of me. You see, we're something extra special to each other. We're best friends."

The Cat opened one eye and looked at Miranda. "Prrrm," he said softly. Then he twitched his whiskers and went back to sleep.